SIMON AND SCHUSTER

SIMON AND SCHUSTER

First published in Great Britain in 2012 by Simon and Schuster UK Ltd
1st Floor, 222 Gray's Inn Road, London WC1X 8HB
A CBS Company

Based on the television series Mike the Knight
© 2012 HIT (MTK) Limited/Nelvana Limited. A United Kingdom-Canada Co-production.

ISBN 978-0-85707-587-1
Printed and bound in China
10 9 8 7 6 5 4 3 2
www.simonandschuster.co.uk

Mike THE KNIGHT

and the Scary Dragons

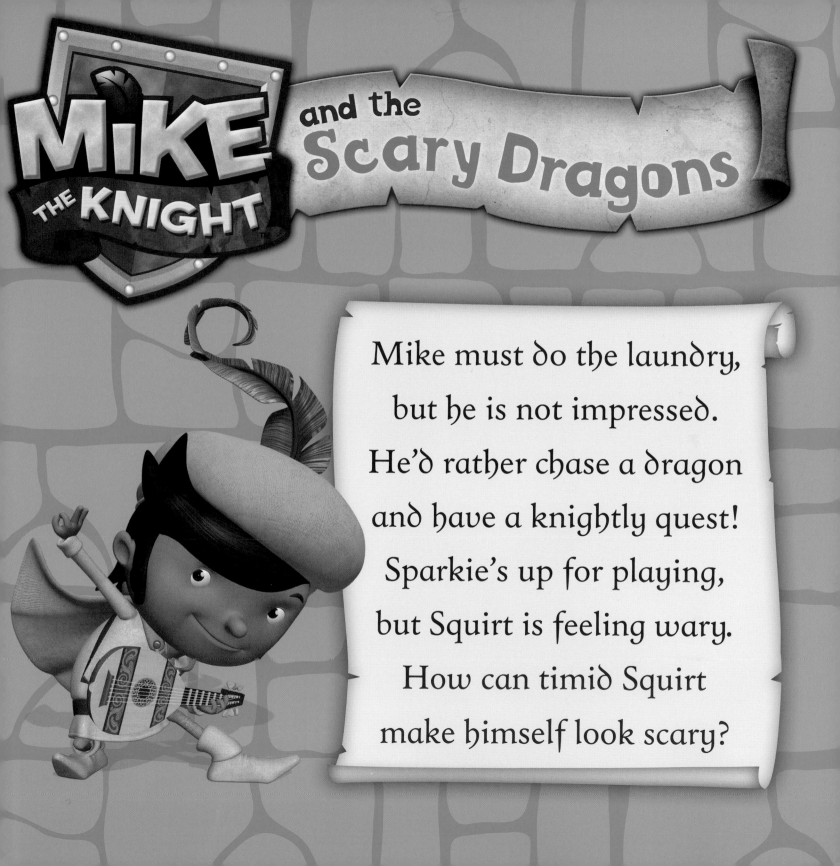

Mike must do the laundry,
but he is not impressed.
He'd rather chase a dragon
and have a knightly quest!
Sparkie's up for playing,
but Squirt is feeling wary.
How can timid Squirt
make himself look scary?

Great knights are always ready for their next mission! Mike was practising his sword-fighting skills against a suit of armour.

"A-ha!" he shouted.

"Mike? Could you bring the laundry in, please?" Queen Martha called. Mike groaned. That didn't sound like a job for a knight!

As Mike marched off towards the courtyard, he passed a tapestry showing the King doing battle with a mighty dragon.

"Look how brave Dad is," Mike sighed.
"I bet he never had to bring in the laundry."

Catching scary dragons –
now *that* was a proper
knightly mission! But
Mike had never faced
any dragons
before –
except, of
course, for
his best
friends,
Sparkie
and Squirt.

"By the King's crown, that's it!
I'm Mike the Knight and my mission
is to catch scary dragons!"

Mike raced to his bedroom
and pulled the secret lever to
put on his armour. Now ready for
action, Mike drew his enchanted
sword. "A scrubbing brush? I wish
Evie's spell would wear off!"

Mike found Sparkie and Squirt in the courtyard.
"I need you to pretend to be scary dragons so
I can practise for when a real one comes along,"
he announced.

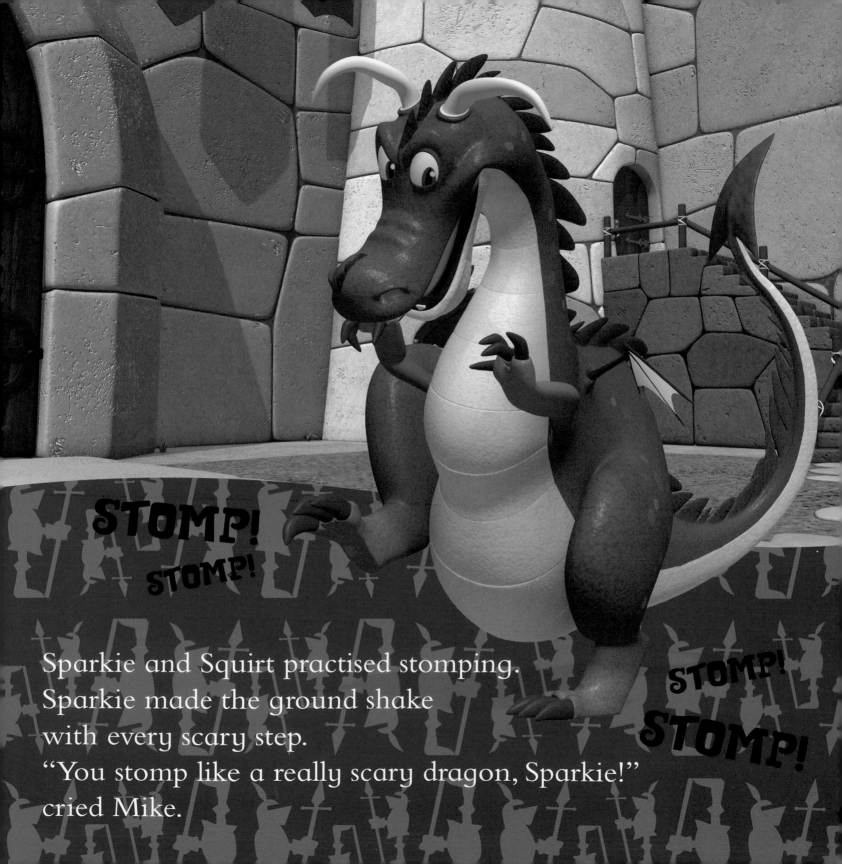

STOMP!
STOMP!

STOMP!
STOMP!

Sparkie and Squirt practised stomping.
Sparkie made the ground shake
with every scary step.
"You stomp like a really scary dragon, Sparkie!"
cried Mike.

Squirt's stomping was more of a tiptoe.
"Not like that," said Mike. "It has to be scary like this!"

STOMP! STOMP! STOMP!

Squirt covered his eyes. Mike looked very scary indeed!

Next, Mike told Sparkie and Squirt to jump out at him and show just how scary they could be! "Boo!" squeaked Squirt, jumping from behind the laundry.

Sparkie roared so loudly, he accidentally set fire to a water trough! Mike was very impressed. "Now I can do some proper training," he announced, "with Sparkie as my scary dragon."

"I'm no good at being scary," sighed Squirt. "I should go back to washing dishes."

"Don't worry!" Evie smiled. "I've got a magic spell to help:

Horses whinny,
Dogs do howl,
Turn Squirt's squeak
Into a growl!"

But Evie's spell didn't work, as often happened.

Outside, Mike and Sparkie were having too much fun to notice Squirt was upset. "Sparkie is so scary!" laughed Mike.

The pair galloped across the courtyard, knocking Squirt into the washing line. The poor dragon was spun round and round in the laundry, then catapulted into the sky!

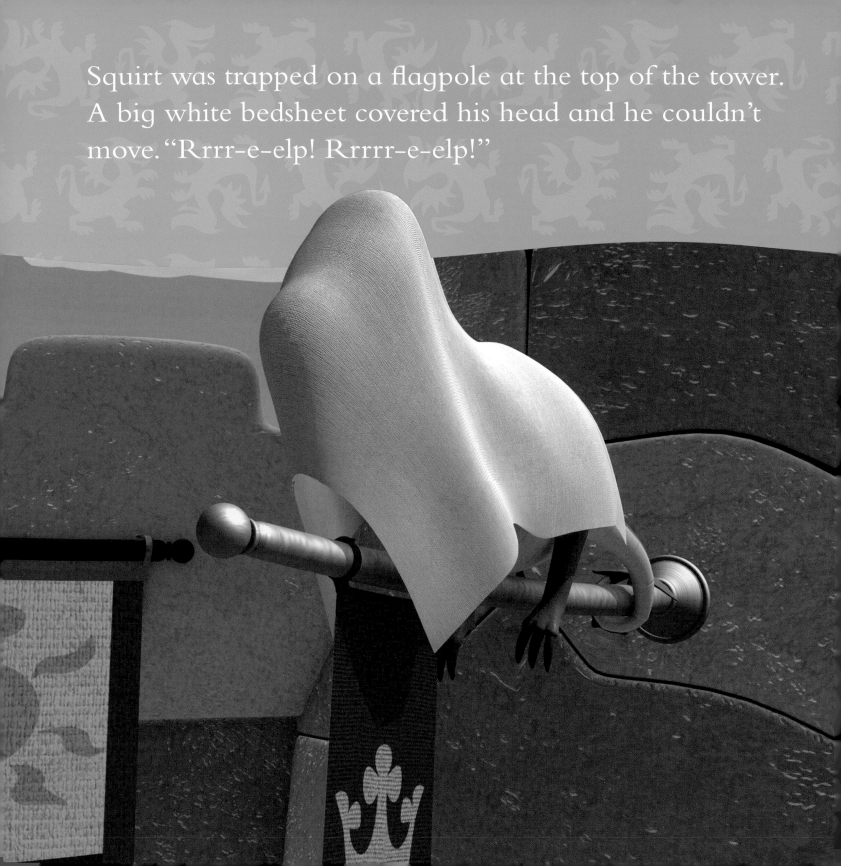

Squirt was trapped on a flagpole at the top of the tower. A big white bedsheet covered his head and he couldn't move. "Rrrr–e–elp! Rrrrr–e–elp!"

"What was that?" asked Mike.
Sparkie squinted up at the scary shape.
"Ooh!" Evie heard the noise and ran out of her workshop.
Was it a monster?

Squirt wriggled really hard and the white sheet fell to the ground.
"Squirt!" Mike gasped. "How did you get up there?"
"He was very sad to be left out of your game, Mike,"
said Evie.

"Hang on, Squirt! I'm really sorry for leaving you out, and I'll never do it again!" called Mike. "We'll save you."
Mike, Galahad, Evie and Sparkie stretched out the white sheet.
"Jump, Squirt!" shouted Mike.

With a big push, Squirt was off. The dragon landed on the sheet, bounced off again, straight into . . .

SPLAT!

. . . a muddy trough! Dirty water splashed all over the Queen's clean washing.

"I'm glad you're safe, Squirt, but what about the washing?" asked Evie.

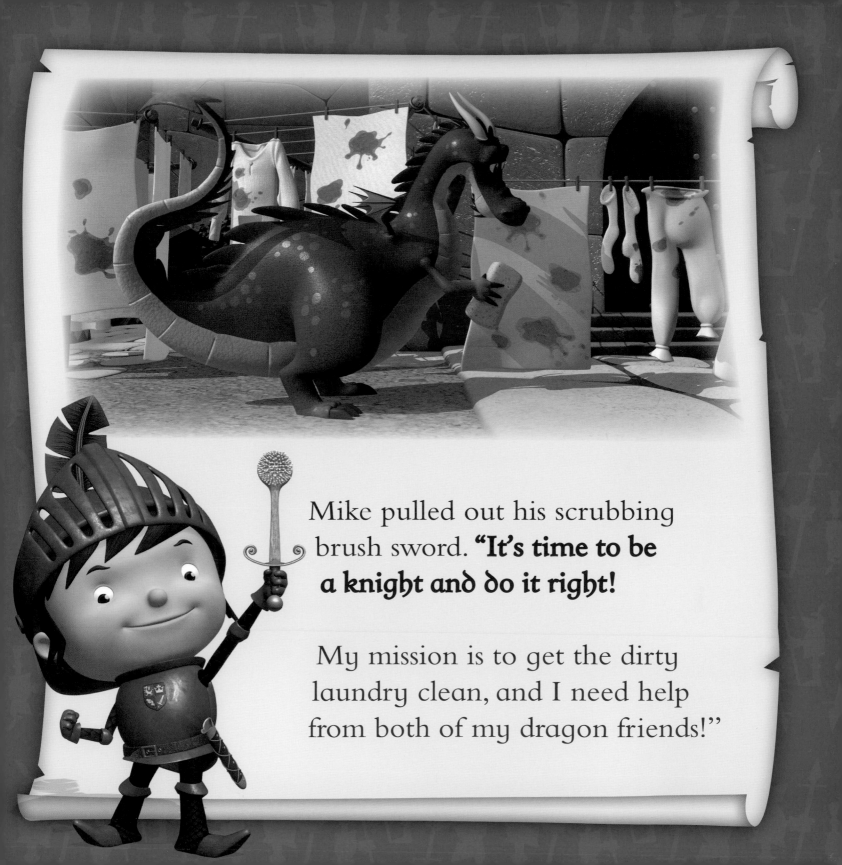

Mike pulled out his scrubbing brush sword. **"It's time to be a knight and do it right!**

My mission is to get the dirty laundry clean, and I need help from both of my dragon friends!"

Squirt splashed water over the laundry while the others scrubbed away the mud.
"That's it!" beamed Mike. "Now to get them dry."

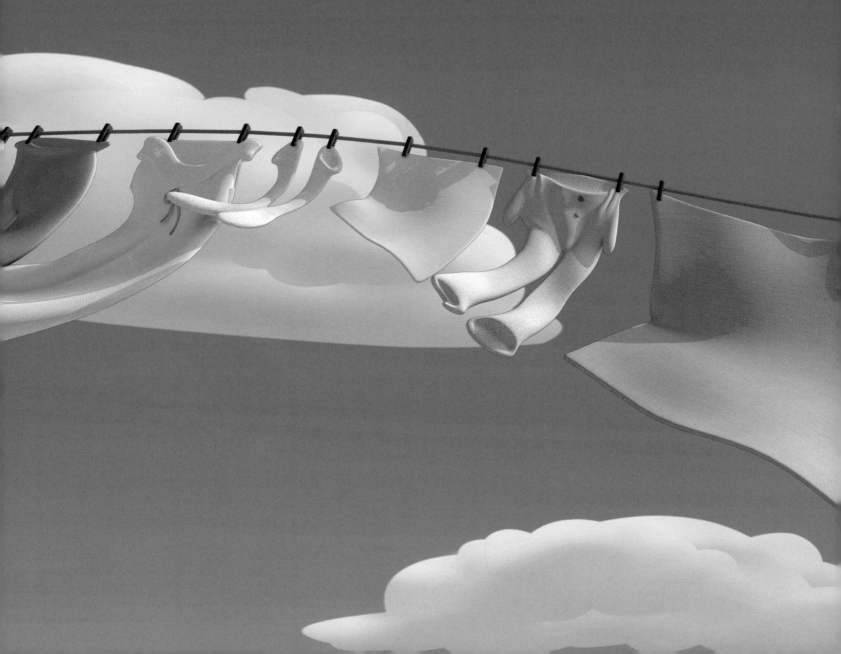

He tied the end of the washing line to Squirt's tail. "Wee-heee!" giggled the little dragon, flying high into the sky.

"Is that the washing, Mike?"
Queen Martha asked as she looked
up at the sky and blinked.
"How clever!"

When the washing was nice and dry, Squirt got ready to land.

"Woo-aah!" Squirt tumbled to the ground! Mike rushed to the rescue, saving his friend in the nick of time.

"Hey," Mike laughed. "I did catch a scary dragon after all!"

HUZZAH!